DR. MERLIN'S MAGIC SHOP

BOOKS BY SCOTT CORBETT

The Trick Books

THE LEMONADE TRICK*
THE MAILBOX TRICK
THE DISAPPEARING DOG TRICK
THE LIMERICK TRICK
THE BASEBALL TRICK
THE TURNABOUT TRICK
THE HAIRY HORROR TRICK
THE HATEFUL PLATEFUL TRICK
THE HOME RUN TRICK

What Makes It Work?

WHAT MAKES A CAR GO?
WHAT MAKES TV WORK?
WHAT MAKES A LIGHT GO ON?
WHAT MAKES A PLANE FLY?
WHAT MAKES A BOAT FLOAT?

Suspense Stories

TREE HOUSE ISLAND
DEAD MAN'S LIGHT
CUTLASS ISLAND
ONE BY SEA
COP'S KID
THE BASEBALL BARGAIN
THE MYSTERY MAN
THE CASE OF THE GONE GOOSE
THE CASE OF THE FUGITIVE FIREBUG*
THE CASE OF THE TICKLISH TOOTH
THE RED ROOM RIDDLE
DEAD BEFORE DOCKING
RUN FOR THE MONEY

*Available in paperback from Scholastic Book Services

DR. MERLIN'S MAGIC SHOP

by

SCOTT CORBETT

Illustrated by

JOE MATHIEU

SCHOLASTIC BOOK SERVICES
NEW YORK • TORONTO • LONDON • AUCKLAND • SYDNEY • TOKYO

ISBN: 0-590-36032-9

This edition is published by Scholastic Book Services, a division of Scholastic Magazines, Inc., by arrangement with Little, Brown and Company, Inc. in association with The Atlantic Monthly Press.

14 13 12 11 10 9 8 7 6 1 2 3 4 5/8

Printed in the U.S.A. 07

To Gavin
From Grandpa

Nick was a boy who knew how to do magic tricks.

He could do lots of card tricks.

He could hold a coin in his hand and make it disappear. Then he could reach up in the air and make it appear again between his fingers.

Every afternoon he practiced in his room. This afternoon he was practicing tricks with a coin. Then he looked out the window and saw something that made him want to go outside.

He saw fog.

He went to his mother and said, "I want to take Bert for a walk."

His mother knew Nick liked foggy weather. She said, "Good, but don't cross any streets in this fog."

"I won't," he promised.

Bert was a small dog with short, brown hair. Nick put the leash on Bert's collar, and they went outside to walk around the block.

They walked to the corner. A drugstore was on the corner. Around the corner were many other shops and stores. The fog was so thick they could hardly see the store fronts.

"I like fog!" Nick said to Bert. "It's spooky!"

All at once he stopped. He saw a shop he had never seen before.

The sign on it said:

DR. MERLIN'S MAGIC SHOP

"Hey, Bert!" he said. "Here's a new shop, and it's a magic shop! I'll bet Dr. Merlin sells all kinds of magic tricks! I'm going in!"

He walked to the door. But on the door were two small signs. One said: CLOSED The other said: MOVING

"Darn it all, anyway!" he said. "A new magic shop, and already it's closed and going to move somewhere else!"

He walked away feeling angry.

"I wonder where Dr. Merlin is moving to?" he asked Bert.

Bert didn't know.

They walked past more shops and stores and came to another corner. They turned the corner and walked on till they came to an alley. Nick knew it ran behind the shops and stores he and Bert had just passed. He stopped and looked into the alley. It was narrow and very dark.

"Let's walk in here and see if we can find the back door of Dr. Merlin's Magic Shop," he said. "Maybe someone will be there, and then I can find out where the shop is moving."

They walked into the alley. It was so foggy that Nick had to look carefully to find any doors. It was even harder to read the signs on them. But at last they came to the right door. A sign over it said: DR. MERLIN'S MAGIC SHOP

On the back door there were even more signs than on the front door. The signs said: CLOSED MOVING

BEWARE OF THE DOG GO AWAY!

Beside the door was a window. Nick thought he saw the window curtain move. Was someone looking out at him? He tried to look in, but he could not see through the curtain. He banged on the door, but no one came.

"Well, I guess it's no use," he said to Bert. "Come on, let's go."

They started to walk away down the alley. Behind them a door opened. A big white dog ran out into the alley and barked. Bert turned and ran so suddenly he jerked the leash out of Nick's hand. He followed the big white dog inside.

"Bert! Come back here!" yelled Nick, and ran after him.

When he reached the door where Bert had gone in, Nick stopped and stared.

It was the door to Dr. Merlin's Magic Shop!

And now it was open!

Nick walked inside and found himself at the back of a small shop. There was a counter on one side and shelves on all the walls. The shelves were full of boxes and cans, jars and tubes all jumbled together.

Standing in the middle of the room was the tallest, thinnest old man Nick had ever seen.

He had long white hair and a white beard. He was wearing a black suit and a black string tie. A pair of small, funny-looking glasses sat on the end of his long, thin nose.

The man had hold of Bert's leash.

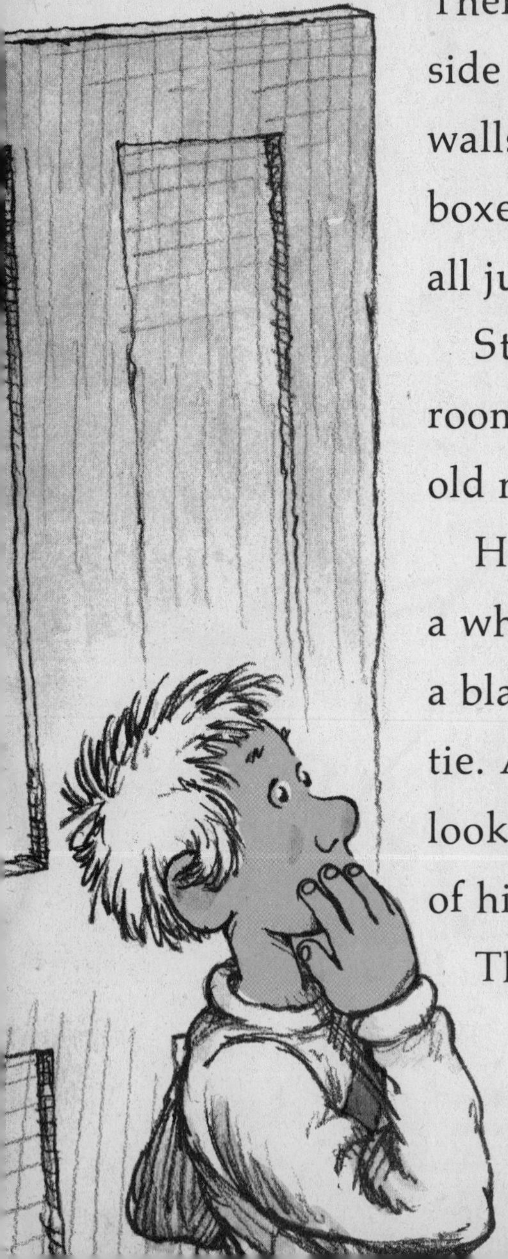

MAGIC
POWDER

"Is this your dog?" he asked Nick in a scratchy voice.

"Yes, sir. I'm sorry Bert ran in here, but—"

The old man chuckled. "You don't have to be sorry," he said. "When I saw you in the alley, I sent Arthur outside to ask Bert to come in."

"Arthur?" Nick looked at the big white dog. "Is he Arthur?"

"Yes. What is your name?"

"Nick. Are you Dr. Merlin?"

"I certainly am. Are you interested in magic, Nick?"

"Yes, sir! That's why I came here. I was wishing your shop was open. I do card tricks, and—"

"Good, good," said Dr. Merlin. "Would you like to see a really wonderful magic trick?"

"Would I!" said Nick. "That would be great! Are you a magician?"

The old man's face became angry. His eyes seemed to flash fire.

"Am I a magician? I am the world's *greatest* magician," he said, "and I always have been!"

Nick stared at him. "Always?" he asked, and started to ask how that could be, but the old man held up his hand.

"Never mind. Just wait and you'll see," he said. "I let you come here because your dog Bert is exactly what I've been looking for. He is exactly the right size for my new trick."

Now Nick began to worry.

"What do you mean? What trick?" he asked.

Dr. Merlin pointed to a corner of the room. Nick saw a wire cage with a small black poodle sitting in it.

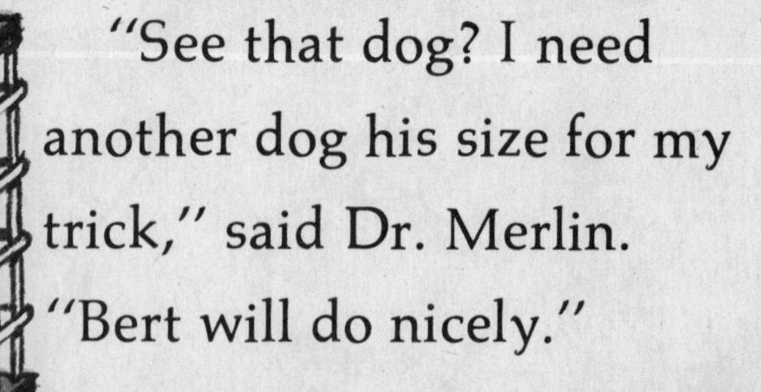

"See that dog? I need another dog his size for my trick," said Dr. Merlin. "Bert will do nicely."

"Yes, but what kind of trick is it?" Nick still wanted to know.

Dr. Merlin put the end of Bert's leash over a hook on the wall. Then he straightened the glasses on the end of his long, thin nose and looked down at Nick and asked, "Do you know what scrambled eggs are?"

"Sure!"

"Well, I'm going to call my trick *scrambled oggs*!"

That was how it sounded to Nick at first. But then he understood what Dr. Merlin was really saying.

"*Scrambled dogs?*" asked Nick, and he did not like the sound of it. No, he did not like the sound of it one bit. But Dr. Merlin went right on talking.

"That's right, *scrambled dogs.* I will put Bert in the cage with the poodle. I will cover the cage with a cloth, and I will wave my magic wand over it. Then I will take off the cloth and open the cage. Presto, change-o! Out will come two dogs—but half of each dog will be Bert and half will be the poodle! Have you ever heard of a more wonderful magic trick than that?"

Nick could hardly believe his ears. And he was scared.

"What?" he cried. "Nothing doing!"

"Now, there's nothing to worry about," said Dr. Merlin. "The second part of my trick will be to change them back again."

"But what if it doesn't work right?" said Nick. "What if you can't change them back?"

"Oh, then I'll give you *both* dogs!" said Dr. Merlin grandly, as if that would make up for everything.

Nick was badly frightened now.

"Nothing doing!" he said again. "I don't want half of Bert to be a poodle! If you want to try an awful trick like that, then use Arthur!"

"Don't be silly!" snapped Dr. Merlin. "Arthur is too large. Why, if half of him were that little poodle, he would look silly!"

"Well, Bert would look just as silly," cried Nick angrily.

Dr. Merlin sighed. He shrugged his high, thin shoulders.

"Well, all right, if that's the way you feel," he said. "I thought you wanted to see a wonderful magic trick. If you don't, we'll just forget all about it," he said ever so kindly.

Nick began to feel better.

"Thanks, Dr. Merlin," he said. "I'm sorry, but I don't want to take any chances with Bert."

"Very well, Nick. I suppose I can't blame you."

Dr. Merlin took off his glasses and polished them with a large white handkerchief. He put them back on the end of his long, thin nose and said, "Anyway, to show you there are no hard feelings, I'll give you something."

He took a glass candy jar down from a shelf.

"Here, have a gumdrop, Nick," he said, "and then I'll show you some other magic tricks."

"Thank you," said Nick.

He took a bright red gumdrop from the jar. He slowly put it to his mouth. He did not like the sly way Dr. Merlin was looking at him.

"Eat it," said Dr. Merlin. "It's good!"

Nick could do some magic tricks, too. He could make it look as if he put the gumdrop in his mouth, when really he kept it hidden in his hand.

He chewed and swallowed, just as if he were eating the gumdrop. Dr. Merlin clapped his hands together.

"Good boy!" he said. "Now I'll put on my work clothes!"

He took hold of a long wooden staff that was leaning against the wall and struck the floor with it three times.

Poof!

Nick nearly fell over backwards. A puff of smoke exploded around Dr. Merlin, hiding him from sight.

When the smoke cleared away, Dr. Merlin was wearing a long red robe and a pointed hat four feet tall, both covered with glittering stars and comets.

"Gosh!" said Nick. "Are those your work clothes?"

"Certainly!" said Dr. Merlin. "What other kind of work clothes would you expect a magician to have?"

He looked very pleased with himself. All at once he thrust his hands out at Nick. His long fingers curled like claws.

"Ah-ha!" he cried. His eyes flashed and his glasses danced on the end of his long, thin nose. "Now I have you in my power! You have eaten one of my

magic gumdrops, and you will do whatever I command. You will sleep. I will try my magic trick. You will wake up walking home through the fog. You will not remember me, you will not remember where you have been. You will not even remember Bert!"

Nick was so frightened he could

hardly breathe. He knew he must act as if he were under the spell. Dr. Merlin must not find out how Nick had tricked him.

He kept his hands behind his back to hide the gumdrop. It was sticky. All at once he felt Arthur's cold nose against his hand.

Here was a way to get rid of the gumdrop! He opened his hand and felt Arthur grab the gumdrop.

Dr. Merlin raised his hands high and bent over Nick. He stared into his eyes.

"I command you to go to sleep!" Dr. Merlin shouted.

Nick blinked. He had to do something, and do it fast. Then he thought of Arthur and a plan.

But would it work?

He would have to try.

He turned and pointed at Arthur.

"I command you to go to sleep!" he yelled.

Arthur flopped down on the floor. He was sound asleep. He even began to snore.

Dr. Merlin stared with his mouth open.

"What's going on here?" he shouted.

Nick pointed at Arthur again.
"I command you to wake up!" he said.
Arthur sat up and yawned.

Dr. Merlin became wild with rage.
"So that's it! You tricked me! You
didn't eat that gumdrop, you gave it to

Arthur!" He roared and shook with anger. "Now I'll fix you! I'll stuff *three* of those gumdrops down your throat!"

Nick backed away, trying to escape the old man, who came toward him with his long fingers stretched out like claws.

Now Nick's only hope was Arthur. He looked at the big white dog and pointed at Dr. Merlin.

"Arthur, I command you to bite his leg!" he cried.

Arthur barked. Dr. Merlin stopped in his tracks. Arthur sprang forward. Dr. Merlin leaped for his life, right up onto the shop counter.

"Stop, Arthur! Down, boy!" he yelled. "Don't—"

But he forgot how tall he was, and how tall his hat was. When he jumped up onto the counter the top of his pointed hat hit against the ceiling.

CR-U-N-N-N-N-C-H!

His hat bent and folded and pushed down over his ears. His glasses were pushed to the very tip of his nose.

"Oh-h-h!" cried Dr. Merlin, feeling his hat with his long fingers. "Now look what you've done! My hat! I can't do any more magic till I find my other hat!"

"Well, it serves you right!" said Nick. "You're a terrible man!"

"I am not!" said Dr. Merlin. "I just like to do magic tricks!"

He pushed the hat back up on his forehead and climbed down from the counter. Arthur stopped barking because none of Dr. Merlin's magic was working any more. The black poodle pushed open the door of his cage and jumped out. He barked once at Dr. Merlin and then ran out the back door.

Dr. Merlin sighed. He seemed to give up. He shrugged his shoulders and spoke in a friendly voice.

"Oh, well. No hard feelings, my boy. Now, let me see," he said, looking around the shop. "Where did I put my other hat? Do you see a hatbox

anywhere? It's just like an ordinary hatbox, except it's four feet tall."

Nick grabbed Bert's leash off the hook on the wall.

"If you think I'm going to wait till you find it, you're crazy!" he said, and he ran out the back door as fast as he could.

Nick and Bert ran down the alley and all the way back to the corner. They hurried along the street looking for the front of Dr. Merlin's Magic Shop. As soon as he found it, Nick was going to look for a policeman and tell him what had happened.

Three times they walked back and forth past all the shops and stores. The fog was lifting but still they did not find Dr. Merlin's Magic Shop.

It was not there anymore. It was gone.

"I guess he found his other magic hat, Bert," said Nick. "He's moved all right!"

Nick looked at Bert, and Bert looked at Nick.

"I wonder where?" said Nick.